LITTLE CRITTER'S
THE TRIP

BY
MERCER MAYER

To Arden Kay,
Doward, & Phillip

A Golden Book • New York
Western Publishing Company, Inc., Racine, Wisconsin 53404

Here is our trip,
from A to Z.
A is for all.
Here we all go!

B is for bags.
Big bags.

C is for car.
Little car.

D is for drive.
Dad likes to drive.

E is for engine.
Our engine is hot.

F is for food.
We want some food, Mom.

G is for games.
I play games
with my sister.

H is for hill.
Down we go.
Don't hurt the horse!

I is for ice cream.
Ice cream for Dad.
And some for us, too.

GREEN
GOOP
ALMOND
NURBLE
VANILLA
CHOCOLATE
ORANGE
PEANUT BRITTLE
GRAPE GUMBO
PISTACHIO

ROADSIDE
ICE CREAM

J is for joke.
I took the car key.
What a good joke.

K is for kitten.
Look, Mom,
our kitten came, too.
Surprise!

L is for lost.
I think Dad is lost.

M is for mess.
Mom, we made a mess!

N is for no.
"No more mess!" says Mom.

O is for off.
We got off the road.
Where is the road, Dad?

NO CARS

ALLOWED

P is for park.
A park where
we can play!
Please, can we stop?

Q is for quiet.
Dad wants it quiet.

R is for road.
We found the road again!

S is for sun.
The sun is going down.

T is for tire.
The tire is bad.

U is for under.
Dad is under the car.

V is for very.
We are all very tired.

W is for waiting.
X is the train sign.
We are waiting.
The train is going by.

Y is for yea!
We are here.